*This book belongs to*

Helen

Howie

# The
# Curious
# Kitten
### AND OTHER KITTEN STORIES

# The Curious Kitten

## AND OTHER KITTEN STORIES

PARRAGON

First published in Great Britain in 1998 by
Parragon
13 Whiteladies Road
Clifton
Bristol BS8 1PB

ISBN 0 75252-526-3

Printed in Great Britain

Reprinted in 1999

Produced by Nicola Baxter
PO Box 71
Diss Norfolk IP22 2DT

Stories by Nicola Baxter
Designed by Amanda Hawkes
Text illustrations by Duncan Gutteridge
Cover illustration by Alisa Tingley

# Contents

# The
# Curious
# Kitten

Some kittens like nothing better than to cuddle up to their mothers all day. They may purr a little. They may lick their fluffy coats with tiny pink tongues. But they have already decided that they will be the kind of cats who sit in front of the fire or on their owner's lap and are perfectly happy as long as their tummies are full and their paws are warm.

But there are adventurous kittens too. Almost from the moment they are born, they are trying to climb out of the basket where their mother is sitting comfortably. Over and over again, she picks them up gently by the scruff of the neck and carries them back to their warm bed. Five minutes later, they are off again, staggering across the floor before their little legs are strong enough to support them properly. They have already decided that they will be active cats, out and about at all times of the day and night.

When Carmelita Cat had her kittens, she knew almost at once that one of them was going to be more trouble than the other four put together.

He managed to fall out of the basket within hours of being

born. Even before he had opened his shiny green eyes, he was trying to explore the world around him.

The little girl who looked after Carmelita Cat was called Cassie. She spent a long time trying to think of names for the five fluffy new kittens.

"What do you think of Willow?" she asked her mother. "Like pussy willow, you know."

"That's lovely," said her mother, "but what about the other four? I think it's nice if all the names have something in common. If one of them is Willow, perhaps the others should have tree names too. What about Hazel, for example?"

Cassie decided that Hazel and Willow were quite good names for kittens, but after that she got stuck. She even looked in her encyclopedia for other tree names. Somehow, it didn't seem right to call a kitten Pine, or Ash, or Birch, or Hawthorn.

"They're not very cuddly names," she explained to her mother, "so I've had another idea. If Carmelita Cat's names begin with a "c" and my name begins with a "c", maybe the kittens' names should begin with a "c" too!"

Cassie's mother agreed that this seemed a good idea. That afternoon, she sat down with her little daughter to make a big list of names beginning with "c". It was hard at first, but then Cassie's mother remembered that she still had a book of babies' names from when she was trying to think of a name for Cassie!

After that it was much easier to decide which names were suitable for five cuddly kittens. Cassie made three lists. At the top of the first, she wrote: "I like these." At the top of the second, she wrote: "These are OK too." At the top of the third list, she wrote: "These are the wrong kinds of names for kittens." The only problem was that it was much easier to find names to put in the third list than to fill the first two lists. Cuthbert, Curzon, Cressida and Clytemnestra went into the third list straight away. So did Curtis, Colin, Cecilia and Cyril. Cleopatra, Caroline, Chloe and Catherine went into the "These are OK too." list, but after two long hours, there was still only one name in the "I like these." list.

"I like it because it's short and sweet," Cassie explained. The name was Candy.

This time it was Cassie who had a good idea. "Short and sweet!" she exclaimed. "I'll name all the kittens after my favourite sweets, whether they begin with a "c" or not!"

And before her mother had time to agree or disagree, the names just floated straight into the little girl's head.

"Candy, Fudge, Toffee and Lollipop!" she laughed. "Those are just the right kinds of names for kittens. The white one can be Candy. The two brown ones can be Fudge and Toffee. And the stripey one can be Lollipop. They're all perfect!"

"Just a minute," laughed her mother, "aren't you forgetting someone?" And she pointed at the floor, where the fifth little kitten was once again heading out across the carpet.

"He's sweet in a way," said Cassie doubtfully, "but not in a fluffy, cuddly kind of way. I can't imagine calling *him* a sugary name, can you?"

"Well, no," her mother agreed, "but I do think he looks as though he could be called Peanut, and that's a snack, if not a sweet."

"Peanut is fine," agreed Cassie. And she bent down to give

Candy, Fudge, Toffee, Lollipop *and* Peanut a big hug.

Do you know someone who is never ever called by his or her real name? Often no one can remember quite why that is. You know, that's exactly what happened to the adventurous kitten. After that first day of being called Peanut, he never heard the name again. And that was because it soon became obvious that there was only one name that really suited his character. From that day to this, he has been called Pickle. And from that day to this, he has *been* in a pickle almost *all* the time.

As soon as his eyes were open, the naughty little kitten set off to explore the world. He soon found the door to the kitchen and all the delicious things that were inside. When *all* the cakes for some visitors' tea were found to have tiny little bites in them, it didn't take long to follow a trail of crumbs back to the cushion were Pickle was taking a nap. You never saw such an innocent little sleeping face!

To tell you the truth, Pickle felt a little bit ill after so many sweet mouthfuls. When he felt better, he decided to explore the rest of the house. In the bathroom, he found that he could nudge one of the taps with his paw and get a nice drink of cool water. Unfortunately, it didn't occur to the curious kitten to nudge the tap *back* again, so Cassie's father slipped straight into a large puddle on the floor when he came in to brush his teeth. He blamed Cassie first and then her mother, until his wife pointed out that *he* had been in the bathroom last. Luckily for Pickle,

his wet pawprints had dried as
the tap dripped.

The next day, Pickle decided to
see what was in the bedrooms.
He pulled seventeen socks out
from underneath Cassie's
brother's bed, much to the
amazement of everyone in the
house who had ever lost a sock.

"I don't *know* how they got
there," wailed Cassie's brother.

In Cassie's parents' room,
Pickle discovered that he could
climb up the chest of drawers
and perch on top of the
wardrobe. It was rather an effort
to make the climb, so when he
got to the top, he had a little rest.

When he woke up, several hours later, it was completely dark. Pickle was a clever little kitten and he thought he could remember which side the bed was on. Bravely, he jumped out into the blackness.

"Oooowwww! Help! We're being attacked! There are dozens of them! Help!"

Cassie's dad had been rudely awakened by a kitten in the middle of his tummy, just as he was dreaming of capturing a gang of criminals single-handed. Cassie's mother, who didn't know *what* was going on, was halfway through dialling the number of the police station before she realised that she could hear the patter of tiny feet scampering down the hallway.

"It was that wretched kitten!" she whispered. "Ssshh! You'll wake the children. You wouldn't want *them* to know that you'd been attacked by a kitten, would you, dear?"

Cassie's dad said some rather rude words and went back to sleep, but not before he had searched under the bed and over the wardrobe and shut the door very firmly indeed.

Meanwhile, Pickle was being told off by Carmelita Cat in no

uncertain terms. She was really worried about her little one.

"If you go on like this, my son," she said, "you will be turned out into the garden and only let in twice a day for meals. That happens to some cats, you know."

But Pickle thought that sounded quite an interesting idea. He had always wondered about the world outside the house, and now he knew that some cats lived in it. The very next day, he decided to explore the garden.

The garden of the house where Cassie lived was not, in fact, very big. There was a patch of grass with rather a lot of weeds in it, a

few bushes, and a path leading
to a gate at the end.

It didn't take Pickle long to
discover that there was nothing
very interesting in the garden,
but it did seem as though there
were places worth visiting outside
the garden. With no thought of
danger or of getting lost, the
kitten jumped over the gate and
set off into the countryside.

It was a beautifully warm and sunny day when the little kitten set out. In no time at all, he had seen a lifetime's number of wonderful things. There was a butterfly sunning its wings on a huge pink flower. There was a line of hundreds of tiny ants marching across the path. Pickle had his nose bitten several times and learned not to tickle ants with his whiskers.

Further along the path, there was a little pond with a duck swimming happily on it. Pickle dipped his paw into the water and was delighted to see large ripples fanning out into the middle of the pond. The duck, being twice as big as the kitten, quacked crossly at him for disturbing the fish. Pickle, of course, was too small to understand more than a few words of foreign languages, so he simply miaowed at the duck and wandered on, although he did think that he had understood the word "fish", and this made him feel extremely hungry.

You must remember that Pickle was only a very young kitten. His mother had not had time to teach him everything he should know. So when Pickle felt peckish, the only thing he could think of doing was going back to the house and diving into one of the six little bowls of cat food that sat on a special mat in the hall. In fact, now that he came to think of it, he was so hungry that he might dive into more than one of the bowls, he thought.

As soon as Pickle turned back to find his way home, he realised that he had a very big problem. He couldn't for the life of him remember whether he had to turn left or right at the pond. Things looked different, somehow, from the opposite direction. He knew that the path went straight on past the butterfly, but when he saw, with a sinking feeling in his tummy, that butterflies can fly from flower to flower, he had to admit that he was well and truly lost. He might never see Candy and Fudge and Toffee and Lollipop and his big, cuddly mother again!

Now Pickle, as we know, was a brave little cat, and he sat down by the path to try to work out what to do. As he did so, he noticed one of the butterflies flitting up, up, up into a tree high above him.

"From up there," Pickle said to himself, "I'll be able to see farther even than from the top of the wardrobe. Perhaps I'll be able to see my way home."

This, of course, was not such a bad idea, but Pickle had never climbed anything as high as a tree before. Luckily, there was a ladder leaning against the tree, just right for little paws to climb.

When he reached the first pair of branches, Pickle had a rest. He knew that he would have to climb much higher if he was going to see all the way back to the tiny garden and the cosy house. It was tempting to rest for a long time in the sunshine, but Pickle remembered what had happened the last time he had fallen asleep

in a high place. When he woke up in the bedroom, it had been dark. The last thing that Pickle wanted now was to be lost *and* alone in the dark in a strange place. He was brave, but not *that* brave!

So the little kitten climbed on to the very top of the tree. He could see for miles in every direction. And sure enough, that tiny house far below was his home. He even thought that he could see Cassie lying on the little patch of grass with her book. From up here, she looked as tiny as one of the marching ants he had seen earlier. Now it would be easy to get home.

I don't know if you have ever climbed a tree yourself, but you may know that climbing *up* a tree is a very different matter from climbing *down* a tree. Somehow, all the branches that seemed so strong and safe on the way up seemed to sway alarmingly now. It didn't help that a breeze had begun to blow. Clouds blew across the sun and the leaves, which had glistened in the sunshine, now began to shake and whisper among themselves. Pickle almost thought he could hear them saying, "He won't get down, oh no, oh no. He won't get down, oh no."

Finally, the brave little kitten could go no further. He sat on a branch, high above the ladder, and began to miaow sadly to himself. He was afraid that his life of adventure might be over almost before it had begun.

Meanwhile, back at the house, Cassie had noticed that one of the six little bowls she had filled earlier was still full. She went into the sitting room and peered into Carmelita's basket. There was the mother cat, purring proudly, and cuddled around her were four little kittens. Cassie counted them one by one: Candy, Fudge, Toffee and Lollipop. Where was Pickle?

Cassie hunted all over the house. She was specially careful to look under her brother's bed and on top of her parents' wardrobe. There was no little kitten to be seen. The little girl went out into the garden and called him.

"Pickle! Pickle! Where are you?" There was no reply.

All that afternoon, Cassie searched, but as the sun began to sink in the sky, she still had not found the missing kitten.

"He's lost for ever," she sobbed to her mother.

"You know," her mother replied with a smile, "mothers are very good at looking after their children. Why don't you ask Carmelita Cat to help you?"

Cassie whispered her problem in the mother cat's furry ear. Carmelita gave a big sigh and a huge stretch. Then she climbed over her sleeping kittens and trotted out of the back door and into the garden, with Cassie following anxiously behind.

Down the path went Carmelita, her tail held high, and down the path went Cassie, not at all sure that her mother's plan was going to work.

At the end of the garden, Carmelita Cat waited for Cassie

to open the gate. She decided
that it wouldn't be dignified to
jump over it at her age. Through
the gate, the wise cat trotted on,
down the grassy path and past
the little pond. The dabbling
duck knew better than to quack
at a cat on a mission, and he
ducked his head under the water.

A little way further on, Cassie
saw a tree with a ladder leaning
against it. Better still, she heard
a plaintive little miaow coming
from its branches.

"Oh, Pickle!" cried Cassie.
"Your mother has come for you."

But Carmelita Cat didn't climb
the tree. Oh no. She sat at the

bottom and gave three sharp miaows, which meant something rather cross in cat language. Pickle suddenly found that he might just be able to get down after all…

When Pickle was safely back at home that night, Cassie made him promise that he would *never* go exploring without her again. But the little kitten *still* wasn't very good at foreign languages, so I'm not at all sure he understood. What do *you* think?

# A Kitten
# for
# Christmas

Everyone likes to receive gifts, especially at Christmas, but even the nicest present can seem disappointing if you have set your heart on something else.

That is just what happened to Ashley one Christmas not so long ago. Weeks before the big day, she began making her list for Father Christmas.

"He's a very busy man," she told her older sister. "I'm going to make sure he gets my list before anyone else's, so he has time to find the things I want."

"You'll be lucky," muttered her sister, whose name was Eleanor. "I tried that years ago and I still

didn't get the bike I wanted …
well, not until I was eight, anyway."

"I don't want a bike," Ashley
retorted. "I'm going to ask for
something much better than that."

"What?" asked Eleanor, putting
down her book.

"I can't tell you," said Ashley.

"Yes, you can," said Eleanor.
"I won't tell anyone *and* I can
help you to spell it, so Father
Christmas won't make a mistake."

"No," said Ashley firmly. "If I
tell you, it won't come true. It's
a secret. Father Christmas will
know what I mean however I
spell it, and anyway, I'm going to
draw him a picture as well."

"Well, don't blame me if it all goes *horribly* wrong," giggled Eleanor. "Little girls don't always get what they want, you know."

"They do," said Ashley, "it they want it badly enough. Everyone knows that." She took her piece of paper and went off to her secret place to finish the list and draw a very special picture. Because the thing she wanted mustn't be just any old kind. She knew exactly how it should look.

When she had finished her list, Ashley took it over to her granny's house so that she could put it on the fire and watch it whirl up the chimney. Her granny told her that was how to make sure that Father Christmas saw her list as quickly as possible.

"It will fly through the air to the North Pole," explained Granny, "and get there much quicker than ordinary post, which has to go across the sea and ice."

Ashley was a little worried that Father Christmas would deliver her present to her granny's house if she sent her list up her granny's chimney, but Granny said he would understand that Ashley's house had central heating and there weren't any chimneys for the message to fly up. As Granny was usually right, Ashley did just as she said, and as the list turned to ashes and floated up the chimney, she shut her eyes tight and made the biggest wish she had ever wished.

After that, it didn't occur to Ashley for one minute that her dream might not come true. She knew she had wished with all her heart and she trusted her granny and Father Christmas. As Christmas grew nearer, Ashley became more and more excited.

"It won't be long now," she told Eleanor. "I don't know how I'll be able to sleep on Christmas Eve, I'll be so excited. But I wouldn't want to do anything to keep Father

Christmas away. He's quite shy, you know. That's why children don't often see him."

"Don't count your chickens before they're hatched," said Eleanor grandly, which didn't make much sense to Ashley.

"I didn't ask for chickens!" she said. "That would be silly."

"What did you ask for?" asked Eleanor. "You can tell me now."

Ashley was so excited that she wanted to tell very badly. But she held her lips tightly together and screwed up her face. She looked so funny that her mother asked her if she had a toothache when she saw her strange expression.

Well, Ashley didn't sleep very well on Christmas Eve, but she didn't dare to open her eyes in case she caught sight of a shy old man in a red coat. Towards dawn, she couldn't stay awake any longer, so she didn't hear the rustling and bustling at the foot of her bed just as the sun was rising.

Christmas Day dawned bright and clear. There wasn't any snow, which was rather disappointing, but everything else was perfect. There were lots of exciting-looking presents at the bottom of Ashley's bed, which she carefully carried into the sitting room, so that everyone could watch her as she

unwrapped them. The special
present she was expecting didn't
seem to be there, but then she
wasn't really expecting it.

"After all," she said to herself,
"it would need to be wrapped up
very, very carefully."

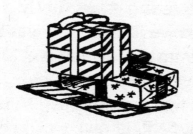

It took ages for everyone to
open their presents. Ashley had
some really nice things, such as
a watch from her parents and a
big book of fairy stories from her

granny, but she was so excited about the other present she knew must be waiting that she hardly paid attention to all the other lovely things.

When everyone had finished all their unwrapping, Ashley looked round expectantly.

"I'll have it now," she smiled.

"Have what, sweetheart?" asked her father.

"My Special Present," said Ashley. "*You* know!"

"No, I don't," her father laughed. "You've had all your presents now. Don't you like them?"

"Yes." Ashley was impatient now. "But my main present is

still to come, isn't it? You can bring it out now, can't you?"

"Really, there isn't anything else, Ashley," said her mother. "I hope you're not being a greedy girl."

Ashley thought they were joking at first, but when she looked up into their faces, she could see that her parents were telling the truth. Her special present was not going to come. Ashley couldn't help it, even on Christmas Day. She burst into tears.

"She's over-excited," said her mother. "And she probably didn't get much sleep either. What is it, darling? What was it that you wanted so badly?"

"C-c-can I say it now?" Ashley asked Eleanor, tears running down her cheeks.

"Yes, of course you can," said Eleanor. "I told you it might not come, you know."

"What might not come?" asked Ashley's mother gently. "What was it, my love?"

"My k-k-kitten," sobbed Ashley. "I was going to call her Holly, because it's Christmas."

Ashley's father laughed. "I'm not having a cat in this house," he said, "and that's final. It will sharpen its claws on the furniture and leave mice in my slippers. No, thank you. No cats here!"

Ashley couldn't believe her ears, but her father was serious.

"I really don't like cats very much," he explained. "There will be hairs on all the furniture and smelly food in the kitchen. There's no question, sweetheart, of your having a kitten. I don't know what gave you that idea."

Poor Ashley! She tried very hard to hide her disappointment and enjoy the rest of Christmas, but it was very hard. She could not forget that by now she should have been cuddling a little friend called Holly. Even when snow began to fall in the afternoon, she could not feel more cheerful.

By teatime, the snow was lying thick on the ground and darkness was beginning to fall. Ashley tried hard to smile as she ate her mince pie. Her father, seeing how unhappy she was, gave her a specially large piece of cake, but Ashley simply pushed it around her plate.

"I think it's been a tiring day for little ones," said her mother, "and we should all have an early night. We'll feel better tomorrow."

Ashley obediently had her bath and went to bed. She really *was* very tired, and her little bed felt warm and comforting.

"I won't forget you, Holly,"

Ashley whispered into her pillow.
When she shut her eyes to go to
sleep, she could almost see a
little white kitten gazing up at her.

Ashley began to slip into the
land of dreams. As she did so,
she heard a miaowing sound
close by. It seemed too real to be
part of a dream, but surely there
couldn't truly be a kitten nearby?

The miaowing sounded pitiful
in the cold night air. Ashley
could bear it no longer. She
crawled down to the end of her
bed and looked out of the
window. She felt sure that the
miaowing was coming from the
garden. Could it be real after all?

Ashley didn't know what to do. Usually, she would have woken her father and mother and told them what she had heard, but she thought that her father might be cross if she mentioned the subject of kittens again.

"I'll have to go and look myself," she said to herself, pulling on her coat to keep herself warm.

But Ashley need not have worried about her father. He too had heard the heartrending sound and he could not bear the idea of an animal in trouble on such a cold night. He met his little daughter on the landing and took her gently by the hand.

"Let's go and have a look downstairs, sweetheart," he said. "It sounds as though someone needs our help."

Ashley and her father crept down the stairs and into the front hallway.

"Put on your boots, darling," said Ashley's father. "It is bitterly cold tonight and we may need to search in the garden. Here's my torch, and we can put the outside light on as well. Are you ready?"

Ashley nodded. She stood on tiptoe to help her father open the front door. As it swung open, snow fell from the Christmas wreath hanging outside.

But Ashley didn't need her boots and her father didn't need his torch. Their midnight visitor was sitting right on the step outside the door, her little pawprints leading away into the snow. It was the sweetest little white kitten you have ever seen.

No one could resist the appeal of the big trusting eyes looking up at them both. Ashley's father bent down and gently picked up the little cat.

"I think you'd better come inside out of the cold, little one," he said. "There's someone here who will take care of you tonight until we can find where you really belong."

Ashley certainly did take good care of the little kitten that night. She gave her some milk and a little bit of minced meat. Then she made her a cosy bed in an old cardboard box and put it at the end of her bed, so that she could hear if the little kitten woke up in the night.

That night, Ashley slept well, a happy girl again. When she woke up in the morning, she found the little white kitten asleep on her pillow, as warm and soft as the kitten she had imagined.

"I'm going to call you Holly anyway," she whispered to the kitten, "even if you do have to go back where you belong. Thank you for coming to visit us."

Ashley got dressed and carefully carried the kitten downstairs. She made it some breakfast before she had anything herself. Her mother watched with a smile and saw that her little daughter was glowing with happiness.

As Ashley sat down for her breakfast at last, and the little kitten began lapping at her milk with her pink tongue, Ashley's father put down the telephone.

"I've called everyone I can think of," he said, "and no one has any report of a missing kitten. It looks as thought this little one will be looking for a new home."

Ashley didn't dare to look up. She couldn't bear to hope that the kitten might be able to stay. Then she saw her father glance at her mother and bend down to stroke the cuddly visitor.

"It's all right, Ashley," he said. "Choosing a kitten is not something to be taken lightly, and there are lots of reasons not to do it. But when a kitten chooses *you*, that's a different matter. This little one can stay with us."

Ashley shut her eyes tight. "Thank you, Father Christmas," she whispered. "I *knew* you'd get my message."

# The
# Tiniest
# Kitten

All kittens are tiny when they are first born, but some are smaller than others. When Farmer Brown looked down at the four little kittens curled up with their mother in his warm barn, he shook his head.

"I don't give much for that one's chances," he said. "The others will probably push him out of the way when it's time to feed, and he won't get the warmest spot next to his mum either. It sometimes happens like that, I'm afraid."

"But couldn't we take him inside and rear him ourselves?" asked his wife, who hated to see

any small creature suffer and
was always rescuing waifs and
strays from around the farm.

"With the two lambs and the
owl with a broken wing and the
duck who can't swim?" asked her
husband. "No, my dear, I think
we must let Nature take its
course. The little one may
surprise us, after all."

Reluctantly, the farmer's wife
left the kittens in the barn, but
she couldn't get the tiniest
kitten's little face out of her
mind. She knew that the barn
was safe from foxes and the cold
spring winds, but she couldn't
bear the thought of a tiny kitten

being pushed out of the way by his own brothers and sisters. If that was Nature, well, it didn't seem natural somehow.

That night, the kind woman tossed and turned in her bed, while the farmer snored peacefully. Finally, she could stand it no longer. She pulled on her dressing gown and her sensible slippers and hurried downstairs.

Outside, the wind had dropped, but tiny crystals of ice were forming on everything in the farm-yard. Even cobwebs stretched across the window of the old hen shed were sparkling with frost.

The latch of the barn door was freezing to the touch, as the farmer's wife pushed it firmly down. It was always stiff, and tonight she had to use both hands to press it before she heard the click on the other side.

Inside, the barn was dark but not cold. Some chickens were roosting on the bales of straw by the doorway, but they did not stir as she switched on the one dim light that swung from high up in the rafters.

Gathering her dressing gown up in one hand, the farmer's wife climbed up the ladder to the hay loft at one end of the barn. She held her breath as she looked down at the little kittens, hoping with all her kind heart that she had not come too late.

There was the mother cat, sleeping peacefully, and there were the three healthy kittens, cuddling up to her. As she watched, one of them stretched out a tiny paw and nestled closer to his warm, furry mother.

There was no sign of the tiniest kitten.

The farmer's wife searched all over the hay loft. Three big feathery chickens clucked in protest as she moved past them. And then she heard the tiniest little sound.

The farmer's wife peered closer at the chickens. To her amazement, she saw a tiny furry body curled up underneath them. And when she stooped down to pick it up, the little kitten was still warm and quite definitely alive!

"You are the cleverest little cat I have ever seen," whispered the farmer's wife, "and you deserve to do well, even if you *are* tiny. I'm going to take you inside and hide you in my shopping basket in the warm kitchen. Only you must promise not to make a noise. And when you are bigger and stronger, you can come back in here to be with your brothers and sisters. What do you think about that?"

The little kitten, of course, didn't make a sound. He was happily dreaming of milk and cuddles and mothers who, strangely enough, clucked instead of purring.

For the next two weeks, the farmer's wife fed the little cat with warm milk little by little. Gradually, the kitten became stronger, but he hardly seemed to grow at all.

Soon the day came when the kitten was not content to lie curled up in a basket all day, under the kitchen table. He wanted to be out and about, exploring the exciting sounds and smells coming from the kitchen around the table. The farmer's wife knew what her husband would say: "If he's strong enough to explore, he can go back into the barn." She knew that the little cat could not stay in the house for ever, so one fine day, she carried him across the yard and into the warm barn. His brothers and sisters were playing in the straw, and the eager little kitten ran straight off to join them.

The farmer's wife hurried away with a smile on her face. She did not see the way that the larger kittens hissed at their brother and pushed him away when he tried to join in their games. They were not really being unkind. They were so tiny themselves when he was taken away that they did not recognise him as their brother.

Back in the farmhouse, the farmer came in for his morning coffee. He nudged the basket under the table with his toe, as he had been doing for the past two weeks. Now, for the first time, it felt light and empty.

"That kitten has gone back to the barn then," he grinned, peering at his wife over the paper. "Did you think I wouldn't

notice? I hope it will be fine,
love, but I'm very much afraid
that the others will reject it even
more now, despite your hard
work to make him big and strong."

"I may have made him strong,"
laughed his wife, "but he never
did get very big. Fancy you
knowing about it all the time."

"I know *you*, my dear," smiled
the farmer. "I just hope all your
efforts were worth it."

The farmer put down his paper
and his mug and went back
outside. Before he returned to
his work, he crept over to the
barn and peeped inside, turning
on the light for a better view.

Just as he suspected, the
tiniest kitten was curled up by
himself, while his brothers and
sisters slept with their mother
on another bale of straw.

The farmer shook his head and
went back out to his tractor. He
set off for some distant fields,
forgetting that he had left the
light on in the barn.

At first all was well in the barn, but a piece of wiring near the straw at the back had recently been gnawed by a family of hungry mice. It began to get very hot. Within a few minutes, the straw around it was smouldering gently. It took only a few minutes more for the whole pile of bales to be blazing furiously.

As soon as they realised that the barn was filling with heat and smoke, the hens and the cat began a terrible din of clucking and miaowing. They could not escape from the barn, but they scurried as fast as they could to the corner farthest from the fire.

Of course, with all the dry straw and wood in the barn, the fire spread at an alarming rate. Flames licked the walls, and smoke billowed out to fill the hay loft and curl up to the rafters high above. There was a smell of burning, and the temperature inside the barn rose and rose.

There was only one place where fresh air could get into the barn. Below the door there was quite a wide gap. Soon the cats and the hens were all crouching against the door. The gap was far too small for them to get through, but they gratefully gulped the fresh, sweet air from outside.

Now when I said that the gap was too small for the hens and the cats, that was not quite right. One little kitten *was* small enough to squeeze through. It was an effort, and he rather bruised his ears as he inched his way into the yard, but at last he stood on the other side, breathing deeply and shaking with relief at his escape.

No one knows if the tiniest kitten deliberately worked out what to do next. Perhaps he simply ran to the last place he had felt safe and cared for. Whatever the reason, he ran to the farmhouse, jumped up to the kitchen window, and scratched on it with his tiny claws, trying to get in through the glass.

Luckily, the farmer's wife had just finished her work and was gathering her things together in the kitchen, ready to go into town to deliver some eggs. She heard the tiny scratching on the window and hurried to open it.

There sat the little kitten, shivering with fright.

"You poor little mite," said the farmer's wife, cuddling him in her arms. "Have those other cats been horrid to you? Just a minute, little one, you smell of smoke!"

The worried woman looked out of the window. Sure enough, a thin plume of smoke was drifting out from under the barn door.

After that, everything happened very quickly. The farmer's wife called the fire brigade and ran to rescue the other animals in the barn. Before the farmer returned from his fields, the fire was out and twelve hens and five cats were all sheltering in the kitchen!

The farmer came back to find three large firemen having tea, surrounded by more animals than he had ever seen in his house in his life, which was really saying something!

"What on earth has been happening here?" he demanded.

It didn't take long for the farmer's wife to explain the whole dramatic story.

"The straw is all burned, I'm afraid," she said, "but thank goodness the barn is safe. And do you know who we have to thank for that? I might have gone off to do my shopping without noticing a thing if it hadn't been for this little chap." She cuddled the tiniest kitten. "And if the barn had gone up in flames, the farmhouse might not have been far behind."

"I suppose that means," said the farmer with a smile, "that we shall be having a new lodger in the basket under the table. And I won't mind at all, so long as he doesn't start nibbling my toes!"

I would like to be able to report that the other cats were grateful to the tiniest kitten for saving their lives, but they still chased him away. Luckily, he was as happy as any kitten could be in the farmhouse with his new family.

# The Mouse
# in the
# House

Once upon a time there was a kitten who neglected to do his duty. Everyone knows that cats catch mice. Sometimes they eat them with a lot of rather horrible crunching and munching. Sometimes they leave them as a lovely present for their owners where they are sure to find them – on their pillow, perhaps, or tucked into the toe of a favourite shoe. But once in a while, you will find a cat who refuses to catch so much as the tiniest little mouse. That was the kind of cat that Mrs Mainwaring had, but curiously enough, she didn't mind at all.

Mrs Mainwaring hadn't planned to have a cat at all. She was much too fond of keeping her house neat and tidy to want an animal wandering about with muddy paws. But one morning, she found that a loaf of her special banana bread, which she had left out to cool, had been *nibbled*. There was no doubt about it. An insect couldn't have done it. A human being couldn't have done it. Those nibbles were definitely the work of a mouse, and quite a hungry one at that.

Mrs Mainwaring was not a woman to let the grass grow under her feet. She set out that very morning to town to buy the most efficient mouse trap she could find. It was not cheap, but Mrs Mainwaring believed that you got what you paid for. She returned home on the bus, convinced that she had the springiest, snappiest, deadliest mouse trap in the world.

That night, Mrs Mainwaring positioned the mouse trap with some care. She gladly sacrificed a slice of the banana bread as bait. Mrs Mainwaring was not afraid of the idea of having to deal with a small corpse in the morning. It wasn't exactly something she looked forward to, but facts must be faced. There was no way that she and a small furry creature with a long tail could live in the same house, and that was that.

Next morning, Mrs Mainwaring steeled herself to go into the kitchen. She looked down at the mouse trap and cried out in surprise. The banana bread had quite definitely gone, but no little mouse had paid a heavy price for its tasty crumbs. The trap was well and truly empty.

Mrs Mainwaring got out the instruction booklet that had come with the mouse trap and sat down to study it from cover to cover. She oiled the springs and tightened the screws. She even tested the trap with a gingerly extended fork. *Snap!* The trap clapped shut with a satisfying sound. Mrs Mainwaring had some trouble retrieving the fork. She felt absolutely certain that no mouse could escape from the steel jaws of the trap.

That night, Mrs Mainwaring set the trap again. She took extra special care and put down another piece of banana bread *and* a piece of cheese, which was easier to fix to the trap. She had heard somewhere that mice liked chocolate too, so she sacrificed one of her birthday after-dinner mints, although she wasn't quite sure if that was the kind of chocolate mice really preferred.

Mrs Mainwaring put in her curlers and tied a scarf around her head. She climbed into bed, confident that this night would be the mouse's last.

All night, Mrs Mainwaring tossed and turned. Every moment she expected to hear the *snap!* of the trap closing around the elusive thief. She was just drifting off to sleep at about three o'clock in the morning, when the sound she had been waiting for woke her.

"Ha, ha!" said Mrs Mainwaring, feeling quite bloodthirsty. "I've got you now, my fine friend."

The scene in the kitchen was not quite so encouraging. There was the trap, just where she had left it. But there was no banana bread. There was no cheese. There wasn't even an after-dinner mint. Not a crumb was left on the polished tiles of her kitchen floor.

Mrs Mainwaring was surprised and annoyed, but she would not be beaten. The next day, she went into town and asked advice at the ironmonger's shop.

"Poison is what you need," advised the shopkeeper. "But you must be careful, of course, anywhere there is food, or children, or animals."

"I'll be very careful," promised his customer.

Mrs Mainwaring was as good as her word. She wore rubber gloves when dealing with the poison and washed her hands several times afterwards. The packet claimed that the pellets inside would entice mice and rats from miles around. Mrs Mainwaring felt that was going a little far. She wanted to get rid of one small mouse, not attract swarms of them to turn up their toes in her kitchen. She made very sure that all the doors and windows were shut before she went to bed. This time, she slept very well.

Mrs Mainwaring got up rather cheerfully in the morning, ready at last to do any disposing that was needed. But the bowl of poisoned pellets was just as she had left it on the floor. None of them had been touched. No little furry body lay beside them.

Mrs Mainwaring disposed of the pellets instead. She made herself a strong cup of coffee and sat down to plan her next battle in the mouse war. She felt like a general, planning his strategy. What should her next step be?

Mrs Mainwaring rejected the idea of trying to hide poisoned pellets in after-dinner mints. She felt that hiding under the kitchen table all night with a mallet and waiting for the patter of little feet was undignified in a woman of her age. She thought about calling in the experts from the pest control company in town, but the idea of their bright red van, advertising their services in screaming yellow letters, parked outside *her* gate for all the neighbours to see was too horrible to think about. No, there was only one solution. She must buy a cat.

"It needn't stay very long," said Mrs Mainwaring to herself. "When the mouse has gone, I will find it a nice, new home."

Mrs Mainwaring set about finding a cat with her usual efficiency. She put up a notice in her local shop.

---

### Good home offered to
# CAT or KITTEN
### Must be lively but housetrained.

Contact Mrs Mainwaring, April Cottage, Codlington.

---

"That should do the trick," said Mrs Mainwaring, making sure her notice was straight. She had been tempted to put "Must be good mouser." but she felt that would tell *all* her friends about her little problem, so she used the word "lively" instead, hoping that a cat who did more than sleep by the fire all day would seize upon any four-footed visitor that scampered across his path.

Mrs Mainwaring didn't have long to wait before her advertisement was answered. By ten o'clock the next morning, three people with large cardboard boxes were standing on her doorstep. She had always found it easy to make decisions, so she quickly dismissed the cat who was "almost" housetrained and the one who was so lively that not a curtain or a cushion escaped from her quick little claws. That left a large white kitten with a friendly face and a young owner who was moving house and having to say goodbye to his best friend.

"I'm so glad he's coming to a nice home," said the little boy. "He's such a good cat. He'll do anything you ask him."

Mrs Mainwaring gave the little boy a biscuit and several encouraging words. She told him quite truthfully that his kitten was exactly what she had been looking for and she would look after it well. After a final cuddle and some strict instructions about the kind of food that his Pouncer liked best, the little boy said goodbye.

Mrs Mainwaring was very encouraged by the name "Pouncer". She didn't realise that the boy had actually said "Bouncer", but she soon found out that the kitten was quite lively. Mrs Mainwaring feared for her furnishings. Had she made a big mistake? But no, this was a temporary measure. When the mouse was gone, the kitten could go too. Everything would be back to normal.

Mrs Mainwaring meant to do her duty by Pouncer, so she made him a very comfortable bed in the hallway and put down some of his favourite food. She decided not to put down *too* much, in case that meant he wasn't hungry enough to want to catch the mouse!

Once again, Mrs Mainwaring went to bed with hope in her heart. It seemed strange to have another living thing in the house (for she didn't count the mouse!) but it was also quite nice in a way. Mrs Mainwaring realised that she hadn't had anyone to look after since her son left home. It was something she had missed.

That night, just as she had hoped, Pouncer and the mouse came face to face.

In truth, the meeting was not all that Mrs Mainwaring could have hoped, but she was dreaming happily upstairs.

Pouncer was just exploring his new home, when a furry little face peeped out from behind the sofa.

"Helliaow!" said Pouncer.

"Hellew!" squeaked the mouse.

In no time at all, they had introduced themselves. Pouncer found that the mouse was called Mirabelle and had come to live in April Cottage when her old home had been visited by the pest control company.

"I don't know why they can't leave us poor mice alone," said

Mirabelle in disgust. "They had lots and lots of food there, and I only ever ate a tiny little bit."

"Humans are strange," agreed Pouncer. "My last owner wasn't allowed to take me on a ship. I've no idea why."

"Poor you," said Mirabelle. "Well, at least we two can be friends. I expect you're like me, happier to run about at night than during the day."

"Well, yes," said Pouncer, "but I quite like running about *all* the time. I'm not really a sitting-by-the-fire sort of cat."

"I hope," said Mirabelle carelessly, "that you're not a

pouncing-on-mice sort of cat."

"Well, pouncing, yes," said Pouncer, "but not hurting, just playing. I quite like a game of bounce and pounce, don't you?"

"If you put it like that," said Mirabelle with a smile, "I do. Shall we have a game now?"

Ten minutes later, Mrs Mainwaring, woken by the noise, peeped round the door and was delighted to see Pouncer leaping across the floor in pursuit of a little furry creature.

"I like that cat," she said to herself. "Perhaps I could keep him just a little while, even if he catches that mouse tonight."

Well, Pouncer didn't catch the mouse that night, or the next night, or the night after that. But he did give the mouse some very useful advice about living in humans' houses.

"They don't mind if you take things out of rubbish bins," he explained, "as long as you don't leave bits and pieces on the floor. What they really hate is if you eat things they were going to eat themselves. You can understand it, really."

"But I only take such tiny bites," said Mirabelle. "I can't think why they mind. In fact, I'm surprised they can even see them."

"Oh, humans have very good eyesight," said Pouncer. "It's not *so* good in the dark, I believe, but in the daylight they can see almost as well as cats."

"Is that right? Well, you surprise me. But this is very useful information. The human who lives here is very nice, you know. She often leaves me little snacks on the floor, in a special little tray. She did try to leave me some rather horrible smelling little biscuits once, but I just couldn't face them. I hope she wasn't offended."

"I'm sure she wasn't," said Pouncer, "but I do think you should be careful about the food that humans leave you. They're generally much happier if they don't know you're living with them. I think if you and I put our heads together, we could find a way of living very comfortably here, without that human knowing that we were friends."

And that is exactly what happened. Mrs Mainwaring grew very fond of Pouncer.

"He works so hard to catch that mouse," she said to herself. "It's not his fault that he never catches him. At least I've never had another one of my cakes nibbled, so he's definitely scaring the mouse away. I shall have to keep him after all, in case the mouse ever gets up to his tricks again. And he's such a friendly cat, it's a pleasure to look after him."

Meanwhile, Pouncer showed Mirabelle what she could and couldn't eat. He steered her away from Mrs Mainwaring's Christmas cake and showed her where the bag of biscuits was that had fallen behind the cupboard.

Strangely enough, everyone living at April Cottage had a happier Christmas than they had ever expected. And I expect they will this year, too.

# The Kitten
# Who
# Barked

Long ago, in a land far away, there was a castle perched on a hilltop. In the castle lived a very sad Princess. She wore beautiful clothes and ate her dinner from solid gold plates. Everyone was very nice to her all the time. No one ever disagreed with her or laughed at her ideas. No one ever laughed at her jokes, either, just in case she had been serious.

And perhaps that was why the Princess was sad. She lived a very strange kind of life, in which she could never be sure whether people were really her friends or just pretending because she was a Princess. It was all very difficult.

The King, her father, and the Queen, her mother, were always very busy. They had to do a lot of waving and presenting medals and dining at banquets. They thought that the Princess was not yet old enough to do her share of the waving and presenting and dining, so they left her to her own devices most of the time. That may have been another reason that she became sadder and sadder.

It was not until the Princess's tenth birthday that the King and Queen realised how very unhappy their little girl was. As she sat in her dress of satin and lace, undoing parcel after parcel, the

Princess never gave so much as the faintest little smile. Gift after gift was put before her. All of them were beautiful. There were dolls with golden hair and sapphire eyes. There were teddy bears with silver fur and velvet bows around their necks. There were pretty little bracelets studded with pearls and rubies.

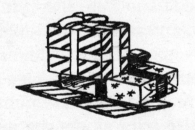

As she opened each present, the Princess gave a little sigh.

"It's beautiful," she would say. "How kind of you to give it to me." But she didn't sound for a minute as if she meant it.

"I suppose," said the King, "she already has a lot of toys and jewels. We must try to find her something new. Something to bring a smile to her pretty face."

A royal proclamation was issued at once and sent to the four corners of the land. Everyone was encouraged to read it and do their best to think of a very special present to send to the Princess. The prize offered was certainly enough to make even the laziest subject ponder for a while.

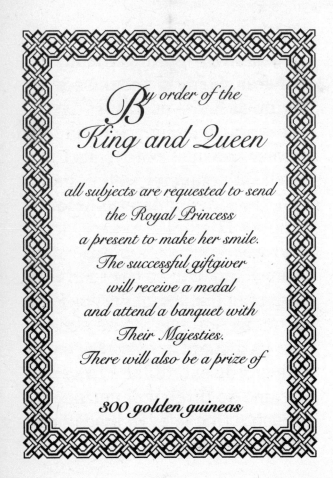

By order of the

*King and Queen*

all subjects are requested to send
the Royal Princess
a present to make her smile.
The successful giftgiver
will receive a medal
and attend a banquet with
Their Majesties.
There will also be a prize of

**300 golden guineas**

Many strange and extraordinary presents were sent to the little Princess. Many of them made her open her eyes in surprise. There was a monkey wearing a golden crown. There was a toy battleship made of matchsticks that fired marshmallows from its cannon. There was even a clown who gave himself, saying that he was willing to marry the Princess later on if she liked. But none of these made the Princess smile.

In fact, the whole exercise was rather a disaster. The Princess became so tired of opening presents that she became ill and was put to bed.

Meanwhile, the whole castle filled up with discarded presents. Before long, the King and Queen couldn't move for boxes and bags. It was like living in a warehouse, as the King said.

In her little room at the top of the west tower, the Princess lay sadly in her bed. She was woken by a serving maid, who came in carrying four boxes and a basket in her arms.

"What are those?" asked the Princess faintly.

"Oh, Your Highness, I am sorry to have woken you," said the serving maid. "These are just more presents that arrived this afternoon. You needn't worry about them until you feel better. I'll just put them in the corner here. There isn't another inch of the castle free for storage now."

"Very well," replied the Princess. "You can go now."

The serving maid curtseyed and left the room, and the Princess drifted back to sleep. It was not very long before she was woken again.

"Woof! Woof!" came an excited little voice from the corner of the room. "Woof! Woof!"

The Princess thought of ringing for a servant, for clearly the basket contained a little puppy dog. He would need to be given food and water. But there was plenty of food and water by the Princess's bed. She decided to open the basket herself. After all, she was hardly ever allowed to do things herself. It might be fun to try it for once.

The Princess hopped out of bed and crept softly over to the corner. She didn't want to frighten the little animal. She undid the straps of the basket and gently lifted up the lid. Two bright little eyes looked up at her, but they didn't belong to a puppy dog! There, with its head comically on one side, sat a kitten!

"Woof!" said the kitten. "Woof! Very pleased to meet you, I'm sure. Woof!"

"But…" said the Princess.

"I know," said the kitten. "Woof! You don't expect a kitten to bark, do you? But I'm not a kitten, you see. I'm a puppy! Woof!"

"But…" said the Princess.

"Yes, I don't look like a puppy, I know. But I *feel* like a puppy. So why can't I be one? Woof!"

"But…" said the Princess.

"Woof! Yes, I know. But I don't *want* to be a kitten."

"I don't *want* to be a Princess," said the Princess. *Oh!* How very strange! She hadn't even known

that was what she thought until
the words came out of her
mouth. She didn't want to be a
Princess! She didn't want it at all!

"But…" said the kitten.

"I know. I look like a Princess
and I talk like a Princess and I
live like a Princess. But I'm not a
Princess inside."

"But…" said the kitten.

"I know. But I don't *feel* like a
Princess. I feel like an ordinary
little girl, and that's what I want
to be, more than anything in the
whole world."

"But…" said the kitten.

"I know. I *can't* be an ordinary
little girl. But I can pretend and

you can pretend. Can't we? If you can pretend to be a puppy, surely I can pretend to be an ordinary little girl."

There was a long silence. The Princess–little girl looked at the kitten–puppy. The kitten–puppy looked at the Princess–little girl. Then they both spoke at once.

"But…" said the kitten.

"But…" said the Princess.

They both knew that they couldn't really be what they wanted to be, but everything would be much better if they could sometimes pretend.

"One day, I'll be ready to be a Princess," said the little girl.

"Until then, only you and I will know my secret."

"One day, I might be ready to be a cat," said the kitten. "Until then, only you and I will know my secret."

Later that day, the King and Queen found their daughter playing happily with a sweet little kitten.

"What is its name, my dear?" asked the King.

The Princess thought for a minute and winked at the kitten.

"Fido," she said. And then, for the first time in a very long while, she smiled.

# The
# Cunning
# Little Cat

There was once a little cat who was very clever, but that didn't always stop her from getting into trouble.

One fine day, as the little cat was walking through the countryside on her way to visit her mother, she happened to meet a very hungry fox.

Now foxes have been known to catch and eat cats before now, especially little ones, so the cat paused warily on her path and got ready to run at the first hint of trouble.

But the fox had obviously decided to be friendly.

"Good morning, Mistress Cat," he said. "And where are you off to this bright, fine morning?"

"I think that is no concern of yours, Sir," said the little cat, "but since you ask me politely, I will tell you plainly that I am on my way to visit my mother, and she will come to look for me if I am late."

"Never let it be said that I delayed you on your way, Mistress Cat," replied the fox. "The service that I ask of you will take only a minute. Your dear mother will not suffer a moment's anxiety on your behalf."

"How, Sir, may I be of service to you?" asked the little cat. "I am only a small cat, as you can see, and you are a big, strong fox."

"The fact is," said the fox, "that I have taken a liking to a little breakfast of birds' eggs once in a while, but foxes, unlike cats, are not such good climbers as they would like to be. I can see a little bird sitting on a nest at the top of this tree. I am quite sure that she has three or four fine eggs in her nest, which would make me a very tasty little snack. If you would be so good as to climb up the tree and collect them for me, you need fear no danger from *me*."

That sounded very like a threat to the little cat. She had never felt so afraid in her life, but she kept her wits about her and looked thoughtfully up into the tree. High in the branches, a little brown bird sat on her nest. She looked down suspiciously at the animals below. This was not the first time that Mr Fox had come by.

"I am quite sure, Sir," said the little cat, "that those eggs have already hatched. I'm sure I hear the cheeping of several lively little birds."

"What excellent hearing you have!" exclaimed the fox. "But that is all the better. If there is one thing I like better than eggs for my breakfast, it is baby birds. They are almost as delicious as … little cats."

Now the little cat felt very frightened indeed. But she thought hard and finally nodded her head.

"It will be a pleasure to climb into the tree for you, Sir," she said. "If you will kindly wait at the bottom, I will bring you the little birds in no time at all."

The fox smiled happily. He secretly planned to eat the little birds as an appetiser. His main course, he thought, might well have whiskers!

Quickly, the little cat climbed up into the tree. She scrambled up the trunk and into the branches, calling to the bird on her nest as she did so in the softest voice she could.

"Don't worry, little birds," she called. "I won't eat you, and neither will that fox."

"I should think not," replied the bird. "My birds are all very advanced indeed. As soon as you get near, we shall all fly away."

"That is exactly what I hoped you would say," replied the cat. "And I hope you will not mind if I make use of your nest, which you will no longer need."

"My clever brood will be able to help me make a new nest in no time at all," said the proud mother. "Nothing you can do or say is of the slightest concern to us, but I should warn you that the fox below is licking his lips every time he looks at you. I don't believe I have ever seen a cat that could fly!"

"No, indeed," replied the cat, "we are not so fortunate, but you just leave that greedy old fox to me. Now, I am approaching your nest, Madam Bird, and I suggest that you and your little ones may find this a convenient moment to take to the air. It has been a pleasure talking with you this fine morning."

At that, the mother bird and her two fledglings took to the air. The fox heard the beating of their wings and looked up, just as a fine nest hurtled down and landed neatly on his head.

"Ow!" cried the fox, losing his refined vowels. "I can't see a bloomin' thing in here!"

"What an unfortunate accident," cried the cat, running past him at top speed. "I'll leave you to your breakfast, Sir … as I don't wish to be part of it myself!"

Alas, the fox's reply was much to rude to be written here!

# Kittens
# and
# Mittens

I'm sure you have heard of the three little kittens who lost their mittens, but do you know about the *two* little kittens who did something terrible to *someone else's* mittens? No? Well, I'll tell you.

There was once a little boy called Jamie, whose birthday was in the winter. One year, he was lucky enough to be given a special present by his favourite aunty. Aunty Ellen, who was very fond of cats and had *fifteen* herself, asked Jamie's mother first, of course.

"Yes, that will be lovely," said his mother. "As Jamie doesn't have any brothers or sisters, it will be nice for him to have a little kitten to look after. But just *one*, Ellen! I know what you're like!"

"Don't worry," laughed her sister, "just one it will be."

But when the day of Jamie's birthday arrived, Aunty Ellen arrived with a large box and an apologetic look on her face.

"I know I promised," she said, "but just look at these two little darlings. It would be a shame to split them up, and they will be company for each other when Jamie is at school."

Of course, everyone fell in love with the kittens at once. Jamie's mother didn't have the heart to tell Aunty Ellen to take one of them away, so lucky Jamie had two new little friends to play with.

"Now I want you take care of these kittens yourself," said his mother. "You are a big boy now. You can look after them very well."

But before long, those kittens were looking after Jamie! When he lost one of his socks and was late for school, one little kitten would find it under the chair and pull it out. When he didn't want to finish his dinner because it was something he wasn't very fond of, one little kitten would happily munch away at what he

secretly dropped on the floor.
When he couldn't sleep because
it was stormy outside and he was
afraid the thunder might be *very*
loud, both little kittens would
cuddle up to him on his bed and
keep him safe all night long.

And it was true that the kittens
were company for each other.

When they weren't looking after Jamie, they were playing all kinds of kitten games with each other.

By the time Jamie's next birthday came around, the three were inseparable. Jamie's mother called them the three musketeers.

Jamie could hardly wait for his next birthday present from Aunty Ellen. From one or two hints she had dropped, he had just the smallest hope that it might be ... *two more kittens*!

"Yes, it's something there are two of," his aunt had said.

"Yes, I do have more than two myself, but I think you already have some yourself, too."

"Yes, it's something I like very much myself."

Jamie was beside himself with excitement. Although it would have filled his mother with horror, he rather liked Aunty Ellen's house, where you had to look to see if there was a cat on every chair before you sat down.

When Aunty Ellen rang the doorbell at teatime on Jamie's birthday, he rushed to the door. There was Aunty Ellen on the doorstep. She was smiling and holding a cardboard box … and it was *tiny*. Jamie knew that no single kitten, never mind two, could fit into such a tiny space.

"Here's your present, Jamie," smiled his aunt.

Jamie slowly undid the box. He didn't know what to think, now. He hadn't the faintest idea what to expect. By his feet, his cats – for those kittens had grown quite big in a whole year – played and purred, waiting for the wrapping paper, which they knew could be used in several excellent games.

The paper was off at last. Jamie looked down in disbelief. In his hands were two *mittens*. They had obviously been made by Aunty Ellen herself, for on each mitten she had embroidered a picture of one of Jamie's furry friends.

"Th-th-thank you," said Jamie, politely, though he found it hard to get the words out. Mittens! Mittens with kittens on them! The idea was too horrible for words! Jamie tried for just one second to imagine wearing them for school. He could almost see the laughing faces of his friends and their giggling chant, "He's got kittens on his mittens! Miaow!" No, it couldn't be.

That night, Jamie and the cats came up with a plan. The cats didn't actually *say* very much, but they always let Jamie know if he was on the right lines when he was trying to work something out for himself. Now all three sat on his bed and thought carefully about the problem of the mittens.

"It will be all right," said Jamie, "in the summer. No one expects you to wear mittens in the summer. With any luck, by next winter, I'll be too big for them, so we really only have the next three or four months to worry about."

One cat rubbed its face against his leg in agreement.

"Mum will want to make sure I wear them," said Jamie, "but I do have other mittens and gloves, so I think I can avoid having to wear them for school by saying I don't want to risk losing them in the playground. I've lost lots of things this year, so she'll probably be pleased about that."

The second cat gave a little miaow to show that she understood perfectly.

"I'll tuck them in the back of a drawer and hope she doesn't remember them at all," said Jamie.

For two months, all went well. The mittens with kittens were never mentioned. Then, one morning, Jamie's mother had a message for him at breakfast.

"Your Aunty Ellen has just called," she said, "and asked if she can take you ice-skating this morning. Will you like that?"

"Yes!" Jamie was really pleased, but his mother had not yet finished what she was saying.

"I think it would be nice if you wore your lovely mittens, don't you?" she asked.

"Y-y-yes," Jamie agreed, but already he knew there was a problem. Some of his friends might well be at the skating rink today. What on earth was he going to do?

Jamie went glumly to his bedroom and got the mittens out of the drawer. They were just as dreadful as he remembered. Well, perhaps that wasn't fair. They would have looked very sweet on a *baby*, but on a boy who went to school and was in the football team, they would look absolutely dreadful.

Jamie put on his boots and his jacket with a heavy heart. He couldn't possibly manage to lose his mittens between the house and the skating rink. Aunty Ellen's eagle eyes were sure to spot them if he tried to leave them in the car. For a moment of madness, he considered throwing them casually out of the car window, before he realised that it was *very* cold outside and Aunty Ellen would notice right away if he so much as touched the button that made the windows slide up and down.

Thinking about opening windows made him remember that it was pretty cold at the rink. He would be glad of those mittens, if only they didn't have kittens on them! Kittens at home were one thing. Kittens on *clothes* were something else entirely. Now he came to think of it, Aunty Ellen did have quite a lot of jumpers with cats on them. It obviously wasn't a subject that worried her at all.

With a sinking heart, Jamie heard the doorbell ring. She was here! With a sigh, he turned to pick up his mittens from the bed … and saw something absolutely wonderful! His cats, his adorable, cuddly, friendly, furry cats, each had a mitten between her front paws and was *chewing* it!

There was no doubt about it. Those mittens were chewed to bits. Jamie could hardly keep a giggle out of his voice as he carried the two soggy scraps into the kitchen.

"Oh, Mum," he said, "look at what those kittens have done to my *lovely* mittens. I *am* sorry, Aunty Ellen. I don't think I'll be able to wear them *ever* again. What a *shame*!"

"I can't understand it," said Aunty Ellen. "I thought those kitten-cats were so well behaved and always did whatever you told them."

"Sometimes," said Jamie quietly to himself, as they walked to the car, "I don't even have to *tell* them. Cats really are the most wonderful friends in the world."

# Six Little Kittens

Once upon a time there was a mother cat who had six little kittens. They were all black, with one or two little white patches.

"How an earth am I going to tell them apart?" the mother cat wondered. "They will be up to all sorts of naughtiness, pretending to be each other."

Before long, the mother cat noticed a curious thing. Each of the kittens had a different number of white patches. The first little kitten was black all over, with one white sock. The second little kitten had *two* white socks. The third had three, and the fourth had four. The fifth little kitten had four white socks *and* a white ear. The sixth kitten, who was the smallest of all, had four white socks and *two* white ears. How very odd!

"Now I'll be able to tell you apart," said the mother cat. "I shall call you Number One, and you Number Two, and you Number Three and so on."

At first, this arrangement worked pretty well. The little kittens were much too small to realise that they had strange names. But when they were old enough to start going outside to investigate the garden and the countryside beyond, they soon met up with other kittens, who had proper kitten names.

"My name is Fluffy," a neighbouring kitten would say. "What's yours?"

And the kitten from next door would have to reply, "My name's Number Four."

"What kind of a name is that?" Fluffy would ask. "I think that's very strange. What are your brothers and sisters called?"

"Number One, Number Two, Number Three, Number Five and Number Six."

At that point, the neighbouring kitten would run off laughing to tell his friends.

As time went on, the mother cat's six kittens longed more than anything else to have proper kitten names like all the other cats.

One day, the first little kitten decided to take matters into her own paws.

"I'm not going to be known as Number One any longer," she announced. "From now on, I want to be called Angel."

"I think Buttercup would be a good name," said Number Two.

"And I want to be called Oscar," said Number Three.

"And I want to be called Tumble," said Number Four.

"I've always wanted to be called Growler," confessed Number Five.

"And I have chosen Princess Priscilla Primrose as my name," said the sixth little kitten. "I think it suits me perfectly."

"Stop, stop, stop!" cried the poor mother cat. "I can't remember all those names! Give me a little while to think about it and I'll try to find you some names that I *can* remember. Now leave me in peace, children. This is not easy."

The mother cat sat on a sunny windowsill and thought and thought. She had so much to do each day, keeping her eye on those lively kittens, that she knew she would never remember six new names. And anyway, she thought of them as Number One, Number Two and so on now. The names seemed to suit them somehow. On the other paw, she could understand why the kittens wanted proper names. She had a long and rather grand name herself.

The mother cat sighed. Like any mother, she wanted her children to have everything that was good in the cat world. But six new names! It made her head swim and her eyes water.

In the garden next door, some children were playing.

*One, two, buckle my shoe,*
*Three, four, knock at the door,*
*Five, six, pick up sticks,*
*Seven, eight, open the gate.*

Really, those human children did play some silly games! But suddenly, the mother cat realised that the song they were singing was a rhyme and that rhymes are often a very good way of remembering things.

With a sigh of relief, she began to work out her Naming Plan. By teatime, when the little kittens were tired out from their playing, she called them all to her and told them what she had decided.

"Number One, I'll call you Sunshine," she said, "for you are so merry and bright."

"Number Two, you wanted a flower name, so I will call you Bluebell. Number Three will be perfect as Felix, which was my father's name. Number Four, my grandfather was called Mortimer. That will suit you much better than Tumble. And Number Five, my other grandfather's name was Cliveman. How about that?"

"And what about me?" asked Number Six. "I want a long, grand name like yours, Mamma."

"Then you shall be called Trixiebell Primrose Catkin, but I shall shorten that for everyday use. In fact, I shall shorten all your names to make them easier to say."

Can you work out why the mother cat chose the names she did? If you could hear her call them in from the garden, you would know straight away.

"Come here!" she calls. "Come here, Sun, Blue, Fee, Mor, Clive, Trix! It's time for bed!"

# The
# Singing
# Kitten

Almost every kitten you will ever meet is sweet and fluffy and lovable. Sometimes, it is true, kittens have annoying little habits. They may lick your ice cream when you're not looking. They may tangle your shoelaces when you're reading a book. They may decide to sharpen their little claws on a soft part of your body. All these problems can usually be solved with a little patience and a lot of training. By the time they are grown-up cats, most kittens are clean, adorable pets, who are a pleasure to have in your home and cuddle in your arms.

Twiddles was a little different. Oh, he didn't scratch the furniture or jump up on the table. He didn't make any kind of mess on the floor or leap on people when they were sleeping. What Twiddles did was much worse than that. He sang.

Many kittens and cats, on a fine sunny morning when they feel that all is well in cat heaven, will raise their voices in a soulful salute to the day. But it is over in a minute. Twiddles sang for hour after hour after hour. He sang long, long songs, with choruses and verses and twiddly bits in the middle (which is how he got his name, because Mr Capella would call out, "Oh no! He's got to one of those twiddly bits again!" and everyone would cover their ears.)

Twiddles lived with Mr and Mrs Capella and their children, Gino and Maria. They were a musical family. Mr Capella played and taught the piano, and Mrs Capella played and taught the violin. Maria was just a baby still, but Gino had joined the band at school. There had been some painful moments when he first began his trumpet practice, but now he played like an angel and made his parents very proud.

Perhaps it is not surprising that a musical family should have a musical cat, but Twiddles came as a shock to them all.

"It's not as if she sings in tune!" wailed Mrs Capella, which was not, in fact, very fair, as Twiddles was singing beautifully in cat music, which is by no means the same as ours.

"I wouldn't mind if the tempo sometimes changed," cried Mr

Capella. "If only she would sometimes speed up or slow down, I think I could bear it."

"It's not *that* that bothers *me*," said Gino. "It's the way there are no loud or soft bits. It's *all* loud!"

This was true. When Twiddles sang, she sang with all her heart. Mrs Capella began to keep the windows shut during the day. She was concerned that the neighbours would think there was something wrong with the cat, or worse still, that she or one of her children was making that dreadful, unending noise.

When Mrs Capella's father came to stay, he laughed at the

problem and told them all not to be so silly.

"You're all getting too sensitive," he said. "Why, I think it's a charming noise. You should be proud of Twiddles. It's not every family that has a cat with such musical talent."

Mr and Mrs Capella were not convinced. They knew perfectly well that Mrs Capella's father turned his hearing aid down whenever he wanted a bit of peace and quiet.

One day, Mrs Capella stood up at supper and made a dramatic announcement. "Either that cat goes," she said, "or I do!"

It seemed that one of her pupils had refused to come back, saying that the cat's singing put her off her violin practice. Mrs Capella could well believe this, as the pupil was not particularly gifted and her playing was really very *like* Twiddles' singing. Even so, Mrs Capella felt that this was the beginning of the end. If one pupil left, others might do the same. Something would have to be done – and soon.

Mr Capella knew that his wife was not really planning to leave home. It was just her way of saying that she had reached the end of her tether. To be honest, he felt that he was in very much the same state himself.

That night, when they went to bed, Mr and Mrs Capella discussed the situation. They decided at once that the kitten would have to go.

"I will tell the children in the morning," said Mrs Capella.

But that night, something happened to change her mind. In the middle of the night, when everyone was sound asleep, burglars broke into the flat. They were planning to steal Mrs Capella's violin, which was worth an enormous amount of money and could easily be carried away.

Mr and Mrs Capella were sleeping peacefully when they heard a sound that was truly dreadful even by Twiddles' standards. It sounded like a ghost yodelling. Then they heard a shout that did not come from Twiddles and the sound of heavy boots running down the fire escape as though a monster were after them.

"Good heavens," said Mr Capella, surveying the open window of the sitting room and the tools lying near the cupboard where Mrs Capella's violin was kept. "We've been burgled while we were in our beds!"

"Almost burgled," said Mrs Capella, for the violin was still safely in the cupboard. "And you know who we have to thank for our lucky escape, don't you?"

The whole family turned to look at Twiddles, who was sleeping quietly on the sofa.

"You know," said Gino, "I've been thinking. You are always saying, Mamma, that music is a way of communicating. Well, maybe Twiddles wants to communicate with another cat. I mean, perhaps she's lonely."

It was worth trying. The very next day, Mrs Capella bought a friend for Twiddles. For the first time in months, peace reigned.

"We definitely made the right decision," said Mr Capella, watching the two kittens playing together. Perhaps it is just as well that he doesn't know that in the very near future those two kittens are planning … duets!

# The Lazy Cat

Once there was a cat who was extremely lazy. She spent most of her day asleep on her owner's bed and the rest of the time enjoying the many tasty little snacks that her owner prepared. She was a thoroughly spoilt cat, which was doing her no good at all.

One day, Prunella (for that was the cat's name) felt rather breathless as she climbed on to the bed. She lay there in a pathetic way, so that her elderly owner became very worried and hurried to take her to the vet. To be honest, Prunella was so fat, he could hardly carry her!

The vet spoke sternly to Mr Mills, who took care of Prunella.

"What that cat needs is more exercise and less food!" he said. "If you go on like this, you'll make her seriously ill."

Mr Mills was very upset. "But she won't eat ordinary cat food," he exclaimed. "I have to give her special treats. And I can't *make* her take exercise. I've bought her all kinds of little toys and clockwork mice, but she just enjoys sleeping so much. I can't bear to disturb her when she looks so peaceful."

The vet snorted. "That's ridiculous, Mr Mills," he said.

"You are being dictated to by a *cat*. Are you a man or a mouse?"

Very much offended, Mr Mills hurried home with Prunella. At least, he hurried as much as he could when carrying a cat basket full of a very fat cat.

That evening Mr Mills put Prunella on a strict diet. He knew that the vet was right really.

Prunella was *not* pleased. Where were her little chocolate treats and her cream-filled biscuit snacks? Who on earth could possibly want to eat fish?

Mr Mills persevered, and Prunella took a very dim view of this indeed. She became very stand-offish and hardly ever allowed Mr Mills to stroke her or brush her coat. But she still did not take any more exercise, and she spent more and more time "resting" on her favourite bed.

Then, one morning, Mr Mills had an inspired idea. He wondered whether Prunella knew how other cats lived. After all, she had come to him as a very small kitten, and he had very quickly begun to spoil her. Perhaps if he bought a lively little kitten, she would learn to play and run and jump like other cats. Mr Mills, determined not to be a mouse, went straight out and put his plan into practice. A new little kitten came home that very evening.

If Prunella had been displeased before, she was completely outraged now. She arched her back and made all her fur stand on end. It was rather exhausting really, for a cat who hardly moved.

The little kitten seemed not to notice. She purred and danced. Then she gave a great leap and landed on Prunella's back. Poor Prunella puffed up and down the sitting room, trying to get rid of this annoying visitor. Surely Mr Mills couldn't mean to allow the little pest to stay?

But Mr Mills had noticed that Prunella had just done more running in five minutes than she had done in the whole of the last five months! The kitten *was* going to stay.

The next few weeks were very painful for Prunella. Day and night, the kitten wanted to play. Sometimes she ended up doing it because it was less trouble than running away! And little by little, the big cat began to enjoy the games of hide and seek, even when she was doing the seeking. Her eyes became brighter. Her coat became glossier. Her tummy became smaller!

But one day, Mr Mills left the door of the flat open by mistake. Prunella would never have dreamed of running down twenty flights of stairs, but the little kitten set off to explore straight away.

Prunella walked back into the bedroom and settled in her favourite spot. Peace at last! But somehow, it was too quiet to sleep. The flat seemed very empty without the pitter patter of tiny paws and a little furry face peering at her night and day. Prunella felt something she had never felt before. She was *worried* about that little kitten, out in the big wide world all by himself.

Luckily, the kitten had not gone far. When Prunella had puffed her way down two flights of stairs, she spotted him playing with the fire hose and hauled him back home with a few sharp words.

From that day, Prunella was a changed cat. Bossy? Yes. Often cross? Of course. Fond of fish? Well, not really, but she ate it to set a good example to the kitten. But for the first time in her life, Prunella cared about someone other than herself, and that makes cats, like human beings, much happier little creatures, you can be sure.

# The
# Travelling
# Cat

Once upon a time, there was a cat who had two homes. She really belonged to a family called Robinson, but they had four noisy children who sometimes liked to dress her up as a baby or an Egyptian mummy to join in their games. Mercedes, for that was her name, didn't like being dressed up very much, and besides, the house of the Robinsons' next-door neighbour was much quieter and cosier. Mercedes spent as much time there as she possibly could. The Robinsons thought she was off somewhere hunting mice or visiting her kitten friends, but as often as not she was next door in

Mrs White's house, lying by the fire and enjoying a second dinner!

Mercedes' double life went on for several years. Mrs White saw so much of her that she came to think of her as her own cat. She had very little to do with her neighbours, but she assumed that they had lost interest in Mercedes. (Actually, Mrs White didn't know that her neighbours called their cat Mercedes, so *she* called her Maybelle. Mercedes had two names as well as two homes.)

Everything changed one autumn when the Robinsons decided to sell up and move to the country. Their new home was two hundred miles away. Naturally, they assumed that they would be taking Mercedes with them.

When she heard that her neighbours were moving, Mrs White did pluck up courage to have a word with Mrs Robinson over the fence that separated their two properties.

"Excuse me, my dear," she said. "I just wanted to let you know that if your new home wasn't *suitable* for a cat, I would be only too happy to look after her for you."

Mrs Robinson didn't really think about it. "No, no!" she called. "That's kind, but we're moving to the country, so the cat will have a wonderful time. There are so many busy roads here, and the cat is out and about so much of the time, I think we've been very lucky not to lose her. She'll enjoy the new place much more."

Mrs White thought of the lovely lazy afternoons she and Maybelle had spent together in her cosy sitting room and sighed. She knew that Maybelle had very rarely been anywhere near a busy road and had, in fact, had a perfectly lovely time for the last year or two. But she guessed that no owners would really want to be told that their cat preferred to be somewhere else, so she said nothing.

On moving day, Mercedes (or Maybelle) was shut up in the Robinsons' house so that she didn't disappear just when they wanted to leave. So Mrs White didn't have a chance to say goodbye. That night, when the house next door stood empty and silent, she sat sadly by her fire, looking at Maybelle's special cushion and feeling very alone.

Now Mercedes' new home was indeed in the country, and she did spend an hour or two the next day exploring the fields and hedges. But fields and hedges cannot take the place of a warm fire and a friendly face. The new house was large, but it was draughty. And it was just as full of noisy children and their games as the last house had been. Mercedes had never been a very active cat, but she decided it was time she put her best paw forward and made her way back to friendly Mrs White.

It took the cat several weeks to travel two hundred miles, but her sense of direction was superb. When Mrs White opened her front door one frosty morning, she gave a cry of joy. Maybelle was thin and tired, but she was purring and obviously glad to be home at last.

A few months later, Mrs White received a Christmas card from her old neighbours. "We all love it here," said the message inside, "and the cat loved it so much that she has been out and about hunting country creatures ever since. Trust a cat to do what it likes most, regardless of us!"

"I do," smiled Mrs White. "I do."

# Kitten
# Dreams

Harriet looked down at the sleeping kitten in the pet shop. "Look at her," she said to her mother. "Isn't she sweet? You can see that she's dreaming kitten dreams, and I bet I know just what they are."

"Do you?" asked her mother. "What do you think she's dreaming about, sweetheart?"

"I think she's dreaming of being warm and cuddly in a bedroom," said Harriet. "She's imagining that she's lying on a lovely pink quilt, just like mine. She's just had a tin of salmon for her supper, and she's played some lovely games with a little girl with blonde hair and a blue jumper, just like me. She's feeling ever so happy and warm, and she can't wait for the little girl to play with her again in the morning."

"Is that so?" smiled her mother. "Well, I know a little girl with blonde hair and a blue jumper who has a birthday tomorrow. We'll have to see if that kitten's dreams come true."

The kitten slept on, and Harriet and her mother left the shop. A few minutes later, another little girl came in with her father. Her name was Rachel.

"Just look at that kitten sleeping there," said Rachel. "See how her little nose is twitching and her paws are kneading the blanket. You can see that she's dreaming kitten dreams, and I bet I know what they are."

"Do you?" asked her father. "What do you think she is dreaming of, honey?"

"She's dreaming she's a tiger," said Rachel, "creeping through the jungle. There's a little mouse underneath a leaf. He can't see her, but she can see the tip of his little tail, and she's creeping, creeping ever so quietly. She's getting nearer and nearer until … she'll *pounce* and eat him up in one big bite. *Crunch!*"

"What a bloodthirsty child you are!" laughed her father. "Do you think that kitten would be happy in our jungle of a garden then?"

"I do," said Rachel as firmly as she could. "I definitely do."

The kitten slept on, and Rachel and her father left the shop.

You can guess what both Harriet and Rachel dreamed of that night. But what do *you* think the kitten dreamed about? Shut your eyes now and dream…